WILL I STILL HAVE TO MAKE MY BED IN THE MORNING?

by

Barry Rudner

Illustrated by Peggy Trabalká

ISBN 0-925928-10-0

Printed/Published in the U.S.A. by Art-Print &
Publishing Company. Tiny Thought Press is a trademark
and service mark of Art-Print & Publishing Company.
Publisher is located in Louisville, Kentucky
@ 1427 South Jackson St. (502) 637-6870 or
outside Kentucky 1-800-456-3208

Library of Congress Catalog Card Number: 91-76305

There are no rhymes.
There are no reasons
why some but witness
too few seasons.

There once was a time,
not too unlike ours,
where two children lived
and blossomed like flowers.

1

They lived at that age,
with only one fear,
between every meal
took almost a year.

Their limbs grew strong.
Their spirits cried truth.
Their joy also flowed
like fountains of youth.

But somewhere within
the spring of their lives,
one's winter came early
as a storm that arrives.

For somehow his body
just simply forgot
to heal itself between
healthy and not.

4

His body grew weak.
His fountain ran dry.
The boy lay in bed,
and he didn't know why.

5

So the boy of long life
would visit each day
and ask his friend
if he wanted to play.

But the boy in the bed
did not have the strength
to play with the friend
whose life would have length.

So the boy of long life,
until he would leave,
would stay with this friend
and play make-believe.

One day as they played
in their own little world
the bed that was home,
lifted and twirled.

Like a carpet of magic,
it rose from the floor,
it flew down the hall
and right out the door.

9

The boys merely laughed
as they took to the sky.
The boy who was sick,
felt his spirit fly high.

Over rooftops and trees,
to the sheets the boys clung.
Again, the boys shared
what it was to be young.

10

The boy of short life,
as if he heard thunder,
then smiled at his friend
and started to wonder,

"Will I still have to make my bed in the morning,

or eat asparagus tips?

Will I still have to wash
behind my ears,

or kiss my aunt
on the lips?"

"Will the tooth fairy
come to visit at night
and leave me a coin
for a tooth?

Will I still have to take
the garbage cans out,

and always tell the truth?"

"Will I still have to brush
my teeth every night,

and be in bed by nine?

Will I still catch cooties
from girls," he asked,

will all my toys
still be mine?"

17

"Will I still have to do
my homework at night,

and practice my horn
every day?

18

"Will I ever be able to get out of bed and finally go out and play?"

"Will we still be able
to stare at the clouds,

will my body ever mend?

Will my birthday still
be once a year,

will you always be
my friend?"

Of all the replies
the boy could give,
he wished to say
his friend would live.

This boy of good health
just silently stared,
at the boy of short life
and quietly shared,

"I cannot fathom
hide-and-seek,
without you stealing
one quick peek,
nor understand
forever gone,
like always sleep
without a dawn.
But everyday,
I never will
forget that you're
my best friend still."

The boy of short life
smiled at his friend.
The boy felt his youth.
He felt well again.

He danced on his bed
as if he for sure
truly had heard
that there was a cure.

"I do not know
just what will be,
or what just might
become of me.
But in my heart
there is no doubt,
I know what
friendship
is about."

The two children jumped
and bounced on the bed.
There was nothing more
that had to be said.

For the boy who was sick
may never grow old,
or live to see
those years called gold.

But in his own heart,
the boy still smiled.
He knew he would stay
forever a child.

MY BEST FRIEND